WEE GILLIS

Also by

MUNRO LEAF AND ROBERT LAWSON

The Story of

FERDINAND

WEE GILLIS

By Munro Leaf

Illustrated by Robert Lawson

New York · Viking Kestrel

VIKING KESTREL
Viking Penguin Inc., 40 West 23rd Street, New York, New York 10010, U.S.A.
Penguin Books Ltd, Harmondsworth, Middlesex, England
Penguin Books Australia Ltd, Ringwood, Victoria, Australia
Penguin Books Canada Limited, 2801 John Street, Markham, Ontario, Canada L3R 1B4
Penguin Books (N.Z.) Ltd, 182–190 Wairau Road, Auckland 10, New Zealand

First published by Viking Penguin Inc. 1938
Reissued by Viking Penguin Inc. 1985
Published simultaneously in Canada

Library of Congress catalog card number: 38-27870 (CIP data available upon request)
ISBN 0-670-75608-3

Printed in the United States of America
by The Book Press, Brattleboro, Vermont
Set in Garamond Bold

WEE GILLIS

Wee Gillis lived in Scotland.

His real name was Alastair Roderic Craigellachie Dalhousie Gowan Donnybristle MacMac, but that took too long to say, so everybody just called him Wee Gillis.

His mother's relations were all Low-landers. They stayed down in the valleys and raised long-haired cows.

His father's relations were all High-landers. They stayed up in the hills and stalked stags.

Wee Gillis didn't know which he wanted to be, a Lowlander or a High-lander.

His mother's relations all thought that his father's relations were very foolish to run and climb and creep around the hills stalking stags.

His father's relations all thought that his mother's relations were very silly to drive and call and milk their long-haired cows.

Wee Gillis didn't know, but he watched them both and he was cheerful and amiable.

So for one year he went to live in the Lowlands with his mother's relations.

Every day he rose early and ate a large bowl of oatmeal.

Then he drove the long-haired cows out along the valleys and at night he called and called them, and drove them home again in time for his mother's relations to milk them.

Once he was late in getting them home. Then the relations all asked him what had kept him and he had to tell them that the cows wouldn't come when he called.

Then the relations all said that he didn't shout loud enough and that the cows couldn't hear him through the heavy mist.

So every night when the mists would come down over the valleys, Wee Gillis would shout a little louder than he had before.

That was fine for his lungs and by the end of the year they were very, very strong.

On the first day of the new year Wee Gillis went up into the Highlands.

Every day he rose early and ate a large bowl of oatmeal with his father's relations.

Then he set out walking and crawling, running and creeping all over the hills stalking stags.

He would hide behind thistles and sit
on the heather and sometimes he would
have to be so quiet for

hours at a time

that you would

have thought

he was a

stone.

Once while he was stalking he sighed a big sigh because he had stayed still for so long.

And the noise that it made frightened a stag so that it ran away.

Then the relations all told Wee Gillis that he didn't keep quiet enough and that he must learn to hold his breath.

So day after day, sitting among the thistles and on the heather, Wee Gillis would hold his breath longer and longer to keep from sighing so he wouldn't frighten the stags.

That was fine for his lungs and by the end of the year they were very, very strong.

So year in and year out Wee Gillis would take turns calling the cows in the Lowlands and stalking the stags in the Highlands and all the while his lungs grew stronger and stronger.

At last the day came when he must make up his mind and decide forever which to be—a Lowlander who called cows or a Highlander who stalked stags. Bright and early in the morning there were two loud knocks on his door.

When he opened it, there stood his Uncle Andrew from the Lowlands and his Uncle Angus from the Highlands. Gillis put on his kilt in a hurry and away they went out into the morning.

They walked and walked not saying a word, down through the valleys and up over the hills, until they found just the right spot for deciding. Then his Uncle Andrew and his Uncle Angus stopped and stood very still. They turned to Wee Gillis.

He was exactly half way up the side of a medium-sized hill not in the Lowlands and not in the Highlands, just in the middle, and he had to choose forever.

Gillis looked down

and

Gillis looked up.

Then he looked

at his uncles

and they

began

to

talk.

First they pleaded and then they begged very softly and very quietly, one at a time, and they politely waited for each to finish what he had to say before the other began.

But still Wee Gillis could not decide.

So the uncles' voices grew louder and louder and they didn't wait for each other to

finish talking any more

but shouted

and screamed

and yelled

until

they jumped up and down and

stamped

their feet.

You could hear them shouting all the way down in the valleys and all the way up in the hills.

Suddenly his uncles stopped jumping and
shouting because a very large man had
come up behind them.
He was carrying something brown and
big, but he put it down beside a rock
and then he looked at Wee Gillis
and then at Uncle Andrew
and then at Uncle Angus.
When they were very quiet he sat down
on a rock.

He picked up the big brown thing that

looked like a sack with sticks on it and

took a deep breath

and puffed his cheeks

and shut his eyes

and blew

into one end

of it with

all his

might

but—

nothing happened.

He shook his head sadly and tried again

but nothing happened.

And then he

was very sad

and

he

said

so.

He was almost ready to cry because he was a bagpiper and he had just made these fine new bagpipes to play on, but he had made them too big and he didn't have breath enough to blow them.

Uncle Andrew was sorry for him, so he tried to blow them but he couldn't.

Uncle Angus was sorry for him too, so he tried to blow them but he couldn't.

So they all sat down on rocks and were
sad together.

Wee Gillis wished that his uncles would
ask him to try—but they didn't, so he
just stood and looked as though he would
like to.

After a long time the large man noticed
him and shook his head slowly, but because Wee Gillis looked so wanting-to,
the large man asked him if he would like
to try.

Wee Gillis said:

"Aye,"

so he did.

First he took a deep breath the way he used to when he was going to call the cows on a misty night in the Lowlands.

Then he held it the way he used to when he was sitting very still stalking stags in the Highlands.

And then he BLEW with all the force in his very, very strong lungs.

The bag filled up and let out a screech through every one of its pipes and the large man and Uncle Andrew and Uncle Angus fell off their rocks with surprise.

So the large man taught him how to make music and now Wee Gillis is welcome down in the Lowlands and up in the Highlands, but most of the time he just stays in his house half way up the side of a medium-sized hill and plays

THE BIGGEST

BAGPIPES IN ALL

SCOTLAND.